This igloo book belongs to:

....

igloobooks

Published in 2020
by Igloo Books Ltd
Cottage Farm
Sywell
NN6 0BJ
www.igloobooks.com

0620 003
2 4 6 8 10 9 7 5 3
ISBN 978-1-83852-152-3

Written by Melanie Joyce
Illustrated by Nicola Anderson

Printed and manufactured in China

Fairy Sprinkle's Magic Wand

igloobooks

In Fairyland, the little fairies are getting their first wands.
"Here is yours, Fairy Sprinkle," says the fairy queen, holding
out a wand. "Use it once to see if it works. Then, you must go
to enchantment classes and learn how to use it properly."
"Thank you," says Sprinkle, taking her sparkling wand.

Fairy Redwing swishes her wand. "It works!" she cries.

PING!

Magic sparkles twinkle and twirl. Fairy Flutter changes a mushroom into a flower.

ZAP!

Fairy Lily can't quite get the hang of her wand.

PFFFF

When the fairy queen leaves, Sprinkle waves her wand.
Four mushrooms sparkle and change into bright flowers.
"This is fun!" cries Sprinkle. "I want to do more magic."
"No, you musn't," says Lulabell, but Sprinkle isn't listening.

Suddenly, Fairy Candycup flutters by. She's very upset.
"I want to make cupcakes for the fairy queen," she says,
trying not to cry, "but my flour bag has a hole in it.
I can't make my *super-special* cupcakes without flour."

"Yes, you can!" cries Sprinkle, giggling.
Sprinkle lifts her wand and waves it
delicately over a patch of little flowers.
Magic sparkles twinkle and twirl.

ZZZZING!

In a flash, the flowers turn into cupcakes with yummy pink frosting on the top. "That was amazing, Sprinkle!" cries Candycup, fluttering her wings and smiling. "I shall tell all my friends how clever you are."

Soon, there is a queue of little fairies waiting to see Sprinkle. Fairy Flutter wants her torn dress mending.

ZING!

Fairy Bo wants long, golden hair.

PING!

"Please can I have a bowl of fairy chocolates, Sprinkle?" asks Fairy Lily. "Of course you can," says Sprinkle, swishing her wand daintily.

The fairies think Sprinkle is very clever to do
magic without going to enchantment classes.
"My magic is brilliant," says Sprinkle, smiling.
The more sparkling magic that Sprinkle does,
the more all the other little fairies want.

"I want a pair of red shoes,"
says Fairy Bluebell.

PING!

"I want a pet rabbit,"
says Fairy Flora.

ZING!

"I want a pretty new dress," says
Fairy Honeywing. Soon, Sprinkle is
the most popular fairy in Fairyland.

POP!

"My magic is fantastic!" says Sprinkle, giggling.
"I can do anything I want to, whenever I want to."
Lulabell is fed up of Sprinkle boasting about her magic.

Sprinkle holds the jar and raises her wand, saying the magic words. "Stars so twinkly, stars so bright, fly to me this moonlit night."

One by one, the stars start to fall gently from the sky.

Then, the stars fall faster and faster until they are whizzing around like little fireworks. "Watch out!" cry the fairies, ducking out of the way.

Sprinkle holds up the glass jar for the stars to fly into, but they just whizz past it. "Do something, Sprinkle!" cry the fairies.

"Stars, fly into this jar!" shouts Sprinkle.
The stars just whizz faster than before, round
and round, making everyone feel quite dizzy.

Then, all of Sprinkle's spells start to go wrong.
"My cupcakes are getting bigger and bigger," says Candycup.
"My hair just won't stop growing!" cries Fairy Bo.
"My bunny rabbit is getting fatter," says Fairy Flora.
"My chocolates have grown into a mountain!" cries Fairy Lily.

Sprinkle tries and tries to stop the spells, but nothing seems to work. "Oh, no, what have I done?" she says, beginning to cry. The other little fairies put their arms round Sprinkle.

"Don't cry, Fairy Sprinkle," they say. "It will be all right."
"I should have gone to enchantment classes," says Sprinkle.
"I've made a mess of everything. The fairy queen will be so angry."

Suddenly, the fairy queen appears. She looks at the whizzing stars and the other strange things that Sprinkle's magic has done. "Oh, dear," she says. "What has happened here?"

ZZZAPPP!

"It's my fault, Fairy Queen," says Sprinkle with a little sob.
The fairy queen smiles. "Never mind," she says, gently.
"A little bit of magic will soon put things right."
The fairy queen waves her wand and says some secret words.

The stars fly up to the sky and settle in their proper places.
The cupcakes shrink, the chocolate mountain disappears and soon,
everything is right again. "Thank you," says Sprinkle, smiling.

"It was brave of you to admit your mistake, Sprinkle," says the fairy queen. "Now, off to bed, fairies. Tomorrow, you will begin enchantment classes." "I can't wait!" says Sprinkle and everyone laughs. With that, the little fairies flutter off to bed knowing that everything is just as it should be in Fairyland.